ORCUS ON 34th LEVEL

Author: Jon Hook
Project Manager: Edwin Nagy
Editor: Jeff Harkness
Pathfinder Conversion: Michael "Mars" Russell
Art Director: Casey W. Christofferson
Cover Design: Jim Wampler
Front Cover Art: Adrian Landeros
Interior Art: Adrian Landeros, Faith Burgar
Layout: Suzy Moseby
Cartography: Dyson Logos

FROG GOD GAMES IS:

Bill Webb, Matt Finch, Zach Glazar,
Charles A. Wright, Edwin Nagy,
Mike Badolato and John Barnhouse

ADVENTURES
WORTH
WINNING

ISBN: 978-1-6656-0084-2
PF PoD Softcover

Table of Contents

I want to thank the amazing and prolific cartographer, Dyson Logos, for the gift of his "The Lost Temple of Aphosh the Haunted" map. This map, and many more like it, are generously available for free from his website, DysonLogos.com. I made some very slight modifications to Dyson's original map, renamed it "The Candy Crypt", and used it in this adventure. If you enjoy Dyson's maps as much as I do, please consider supporting him by joining his Patreon.

I also want to thank the amazing James M. Spahn for creating such a wonderful toy in the Orcus' Claws and the Crueltide Elves. They were so much fun to play with; I hope my joy is felt by all who read or play this adventure. And finally, I want to say "thank you" to Edwin Nagy for inviting me to write this fun adventure. I was instantly captivated by this idea and it consumed for the twenty days it took me to write it. I was a man possessed by the raging and blood-drenched holiday spirit that oozes from Orcus' Claws. I am forever a changed man — somebody help me, please.

Enjoy!

—Jon Hook

ORCUS ON 34th LEVEL

By Jon Hook

A Pathfinder adventure for 4 to 6 adventurers of levels 7-9.

Orcus on 34th Level is a self-contained dungeon crawl adventure for 4–6 adventurers of levels 7–9. Recently, the adventurers heard a rumor that jolly ol' Orcus' Claws is preparing to free his wife, Nohell Claws, from a remote dimension where she has been trapped for a thousand years. The ritual can be performed only when the constellation of Gorgon Major is in ascension and the Northern Azure Star shines over the village of Newville. That time is nigh, and if the adventurers fail to stop the ritual, then all *Nohell* is going to break loose!

BEGINNING THE ADVENTURE

For centuries, Orcus' Claws has pined for his one true soul-be-damned mate, a succubus known as Nohell. She is trapped in a null dimension, powerless to affect her own escape, spending a millennium in solitude. But now, as the time of her return draws near, Orcus' Claws has returned to the Candy Crypt, his lair deep within Mount Strumpet. While Orcus' Claws, his Crueltide elves, and the Naughty prepare the candy factory, Mr. Giggles, Claws' demonic astrologer, is conducting the summoning ritual.

The Candy Crypt is intended to be the 34th level of a mega-dungeon; insert it into any dungeon or run it as an isolated subterranean location. The adventurers either stumble upon the Candy Crypt by accident or they may be sent there to thwart Nohell's return. If a local noble hired them, they are promised a reward of 5,000 gp each.

As the adventurers descend the spiral staircase that leads to **Room 1**, they hear music echoing through crypt. You are encouraged to play the instrumental song *Christmas Eve Sarajevo* by the Trans-Siberian Orchestra as the game is played. The author wrote lyrics for the song that can be heard echoing through the crypt as well. About one minute after the song begins, and just as the orchestra begins to swell, sing the following lyrics:

As he flew over the countryside

He listened for your cries,

When from a little village below

He heard the screams arise,

And there he dove to drink in the sight

And bathed in the blood of so many lives!

THE CANDY CRYPT

GENERAL HALLWAYS

Unless they are otherwise described, the constructed hallways within the Candy Crypt are 10 feet wide and 12 feet high. The walls and ceiling are expertly crafted stone and mortar; the floors are mortared cobblestone. Wall scones with lit torches are spaced every 40 feet. If no specific decorations are described, the walls and ceiling have a color like pale sand, but the cobblestones used in the floor are a multitude of hues in rose, amber, umber, and chocolate.

ROOM 1: WINDOW SHOPPING

The characters see an amazing sight as they enter this room, as their reflections repeat to infinity in every direction. Every character must make a DC 20 Will saving throw to avoid being shaken by the infinite reflections.

Three reflection ghosts are trapped within this room, one inside each column. A fourth ghost used to be in the room, but one of the columns was destroyed, releasing the ghost and allowing it to escape. Each column is also linked to one of the room's four doors; if anyone whispers the secret name of the ghost tied to that particular door, it opens. If a ghost escapes the room, the associated door is permanently unlocked. While locked, nothing — no spell or blade — can harm or unlock the door.

THE CANDY CRYPT
1 Square - 5 Feet
Thanks to Dyson Logos
for the original map
1
2
3
4
5
6
7
8
9
10
11
12
x 13 x   x
14
15
s
16
17
x
18
19

Reflection ghosts are invisible, immaterial, and intangible; they cannot be harmed, nor can they harm anyone as a ghost. However, a reflection ghost can manifest as a mirror image opposite any character that touches any reflective surface (walking does not count as touching a surface). Up to three mirrored manifestations can appear in this room, one from each intact column. A manifested reflection steps out of the mirror to battle its counterpart, fully equipped with all the character's gear and abilities, including hit points. If the mirror manifestation is destroyed, the reflection ghost returns to its column, until it manifests again.

Each column has 35 hit points and hardness 8 and is linked to a different doorway. If a column is destroyed, it unlocks the connected doorway. The southwest column is linked to the door on the west wall, the northeast column to the door on the east wall, and the southeast column to the door on the south wall. The shattered northwest column was linked to the door on the north wall; that door unlocked when the column was destroyed. Unfortunately, destroying the columns also weakens the structural integrity of the chamber. The ceiling has a 20% cumulative chance of collapsing during any intense fighting for each column that is destroyed; if all three remaining columns are destroyed, there's an 80% chance of collapse (don't forget the 20% chance for the already destroyed column). Characters must make a DC 20 Reflex saving throw to escape the room if the ceiling collapses. On a failed save, the character takes 3d6 bludgeoning and piercing damage from falling stones and shards of mirror.

If the characters don't touch any reflective surfaces, it is possible for them to exit the room through the unlocked door in the north wall without manifesting any of the trapped reflection ghosts.

Room 2: Christmas Wishing Well

This long hallway features two large niches near **Room 1**. Each niche is filled with chains dangling from the ceiling, with 3d4 corpses hanging from the hooks. The corpses are soft and wet, but instead of smelling like death, each one smells like strawberries, sugarplums, peaches, and honeysuckle. Each corpse is dressed in tattered undergarments; none of the corpses has any treasure.

The hallway features an eastward branch that caved in. Rubble completely blocks the passage, with 15 feet of debris separating this hallway from **Room 9**. Characters with stonecunning or an appropriate background can easily assess the rubble and see that with enough time it is possible to clear the way. It takes 10 hours for a single character to dig through the rubble; divide the time by the number of characters to determine how long it takes to clear the branch.

An eerie beam of light shines down from the ceiling directly over the fountain at the far northern end of the hallway. The marbled fountain has two basins: a small basin on a slim pedestal standing over a larger basin. Water cascades out of the upper basin and falls into the lower basin. A marble sculpture of crossed and bloodied candy canes stands upright in the center of the upper basin. The lower basin is lined with jagged, rusty nails, and its edge is stained dark brown with old blood. Swimming around inside the lower basin are small spheres of light that cast a dull yellow glow. The tiny balls of light move like goldfish.

The little glowing balls of light are nearly impossible to catch. The only way to catch a ball of light is for characters to stab their hands on the rusty nails, taking 1d4 piercing damage, and then plunge their bleeding hands into the water. If this is done, a glowing ball swims directly into the open wound and buries itself in the character's flesh. The glowing ball is absorbed, and the character must make a DC 20 Will saving throw. Nothing happens on a successful save. If a character fails the saving throw, however, his or her alignment changes to Chaotic. If the character's alignment is already Chaotic, he or she is granted one wish (as per a *wish* spell). Any single Chaotic character may receive only one wish, and any attempt to gain a second results in 3d6 hooked chains grabbing the character and dealing 1d6 piercing damage per hook. The character's body is lifted up and pulled into one of the niches near **Room 1**. The character's corpse is stored until it can be processed into candy.

Room 3: Dead Letter Office

The creature is a **mistletroll**. Its job is to write threatening letters to children promising that Orcus' Claws will sneak into their homes and steal them away from their parents to convert them into the Naughty so they can serve in Claws' Candy Crypt for all eternity. If the characters search the mistletroll's desk, they discover a small chest with 3d10 gp.

Mistletroll   **CR 3**
XP 800
hp 30 (Pathfinder Roleplaying Game Bestiary 3, "Troll, Moss")

Room 4: Hot from the Oven

When the characters enter this room, 20 **gingersnap men** are busy making more cookie-men. Ten gingersnap men are working at the metal tables as they shape raw ginger cookie dough into new cookie-men; five gingersnap men are stirring a large bowl of raw cookie dough batter together in the northeast corner, and five gingersnap men are working in front of the oven. The oven workers insert raw, lifeless cookie-men and extract brand-new, fully baked and animated gingersnap men.

The clay oven is fueled by hellfire. Any non-gingersnap man that starts its turn in the oven or enters it for the first time on its turn must make a DC 18 Fortitude saving throw. The creature takes 10d6 fire damage on a failed saving throw and half as much on a success. Five new gingersnap men exit the oven every third combat round, even if they must crawl out on their own. The gingersnap men ignore the characters as long as they do not attempt to leave this room through the door that leads to the cavernous areas of **Rooms 5**, **6**, and **7**, and as long as they do not interfere with their baking operation. The oven has a pair of metal doors that can be closed over the fiery opening. If the oven doors are closed and magically locked (by casting *arcane lock*, for example), the oven fires are snuffed out in 2d6 rounds.

Gingersnap Man (20)   **CR 1/2**
XP 200
hp 6 (Appendix A: New Monsters, "Gingersnap Man")

The statue of Orcus' Claws has a pair of precious rubies for eyes. Each ruby is worth 150 gp. The statue is magically trapped. If anyone touches either ruby eye, that person is teleported into the oven. *Detect magic* informs the spellcaster that the ruby eyes are magical with an aura of conjuration, but does not reveal the exact nature of the trap. The trap was originally cast by Orcus' Claws' astrologer, Mr. Giggles.

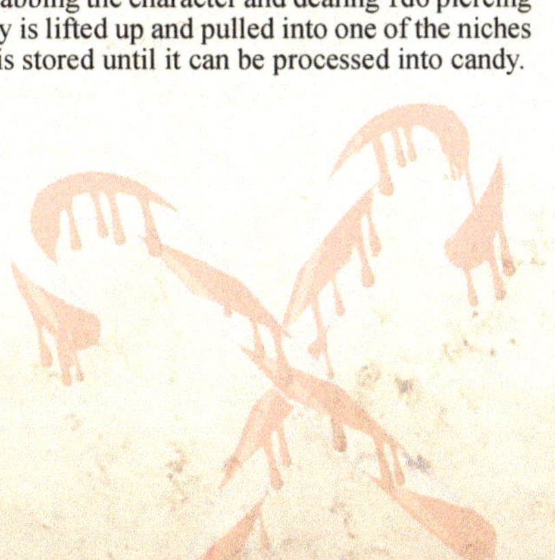

Room 5: Ice Cream Quarry

The temperature drops dramatically as you enter this cavernous area, causing your breath to exhale as a cloud of warm vapor. The walls and floors sparkle with ice crystals, and the entire cavern is composed of ice cream. You see a quarry pit filled with gingersnap men toiling away as they excavate chunks of chocolate ore and veins of caramel from the ice cream walls. Flying over the gingersnap men, directing their work, is a trio of large demonic-looking snowy owls.

The gingersnap men baked in **Room 4** are sent to the ice cream quarry to work. **Gingersnap men** are a mindless race; it is thus impossible for the characters to stoke a rebellion in them. When the adventurers enter, 15 gingersnap men are working in the quarry. The gingersnap men ignore the characters; they attack only if their work is interrupted. On the other hand, the three demonic owls, also known as **kringkuks**, attack the adventurers on sight. The kringkuks have a quota of ore to collect, and they do not allow the characters to threaten their work schedule.

Gingersnap Man (15)   **CR 1/2**
XP 200
hp 6 (Appendix A: New Monsters, "Gingersnap Man")

Kringkuk (3)   **CR 4**
XP 1,200
hp 38 (Appendix A: New Monsters, "Demon, Kringkuk")

The gingersnap men collect ore and place it in carts that are wheeled to **Room 7** for processing. One of the carts currently parked in an alcove along the eastern wall of the cavern contains some other ore the gingersnap men discovered, including 3d20 ingots of gold "*sprinkles*." Each ingot is worth 10 gp. An intelligent dagger named *Frost Fang* (see **Appendix B: New Magic Items**) is also in the cart; the blade was unable to communicate with the mindless gingersnap men. The gingersnap men also found a large magical gem known as an *ice storm sapphire* (see **Appendix B: New Magic Items**).

Room 6: Chocolate Falls

The cavern's ceiling here is 60 feet high. From high above, a fountain of chocolate spews out and falls into a pool of chocolate below. Several large chunks of dark chocolate fudge float in the pool of light-brown milk chocolate.

None of the gingersnap men works near the chocolate pool. Several large boulder-like scoops of ice cream near the pool provide cover for the characters if they choose to hide near the pool. Characters who drink the liquid chocolate satiate their hunger for a full day. If the characters spend more than five minutes near the pool's edge, the **chocolate pudding** emerges and attacks.

Chocolate Pudding   **CR 7**
XP 3,200
hp 105 (Pathfinder Roleplaying Game Bestiary, "Black Pudding")

Room 7: Ore Processing

The gingersnap men push carts of candied ore to a basket at the base of the cliff wall below the processing station. The gingersnap men transfer the ore from the cart to the basket, which is then pulled up to the processing station by Crueltide elves. The elves unload the basket, sort the ore, and load it onto conveyer belts that carry the ore through a small tunnel in the eastern wall.

Eight **Crueltide elves** sing the haunting carol the adventurers first heard as they descended into **Room 1**. The elves are sorting the ore mined by the gingersnap men into different piles. The ore is loaded onto a conveyer belt system that runs through small tunnels dug through the east wall to deliver the ore to the Bittersweet Treats chamber (**Room 14**).

The conveyer belt tunnel is exceedingly small; only a Small or smaller creature can fit through the tunnel. The tunnel is incredibly claustrophobic, and anyone attempting to travel through the conveyer belt tunnel must make a DC 15 Fortitude saving throw every 30 feet or lose 1 hit point due to asphyxiation.

Crueltide Elf (8)   CR 1
XP 400
hp 9 (Appendix A: New Monsters, "Crueltide Elf")

The Crueltide elves are focused on their work and most likely do not notice the characters until they enter their work area. Each Crueltide elf carries 1d2 items from the **Crueltide Contraptions Chart**, a pocketful of 2d6 miniature candy canes, and a fire poker.

Room 8: Bubblegum Refuse

A half dozen shovel-wielding **Crueltide elves** are working in this room. Several piles of broken toys, pieces of warped candy, crumbled cookies, and other heaping piles of junk are scattered about the room. The demonic elves are shoveling the debris into a sunken area in the northwest corner of the room where a large pink sphere is located in the lower section of the room. The rubbery-looking sphere warbles as the junk the elves keep shoveling penetrates its elastic skin.

This is the disposal room. Anything broken or no longer useful is chucked into the **bubblegum sphere** for the creature to consume. Each Crueltide elf in this room carries a shovel and 1d2 items from the **Crueltide Contraptions Chart**. Many precious items were discarded by mistake; each character who searches through the piles of refuse may roll once on the **Random Treasure Table** below. Each treasure can be found only once; reroll all duplicate results.

The large pink bubblegum sphere is ravenous and must be continually fed by the Crueltide elves. If the feeding ceases, the bubblegum sphere lifts off from the dais it is sitting on and floats into the room to attack anyone threatening its constant food supply.

Bubblegum Sphere   CR 2
XP 600
hp 20 (Appendix A: New Monsters, "Bubbegum Sphere")

Crueltide Elf (6)   CR 1
XP 400
hp 9 (Appendix A: New Monsters, "Crueltide Elf")

1d12	Result
1	A small sack with 3d10 gold coins.
2	A quiver with 2d4 arrows. Each arrowhead glows a soft green. Each enchanted arrow bestows a +2 bonus to hit and damage rolls, but this quiver is in the junkpile for a reason: The arrows are unstable. Each time one of these arrows is nocked and drawn, roll 1d6: On a 1, the arrow explodes in the archer's hands and inflicts 1d6 + 2 force damage to the archer and destroys the bow.
3	A small sack with 2d3 tiny gemstones (diamonds, emeralds, rubies, and sapphires); each gem is worth 50 gp.
4	A small figurine of a silver raven — a *figurine of wondrous power (silver raven)*.
5	A small, unlocked box from which leaks thin tendrils of vapor that have an acrid, electrical smell. The box is not trapped, but the object inside — a large diamond containing an enchanted lightning bolt — is unstable. If the box is opened, the lightning bolt automatically discharges. Everyone within 10 feet must make a DC 15 Reflex saving throw, taking 5d6 electricity damage on a failure or half as much on a success. Once the lightning bolt discharges, the diamond is no longer enchanted but is still worth 600 gp.
6	A small sack with 2d12 gold coins and a golden ring etched with an image of a skeleton. It is a *ring of X-ray vision*.
7	A filthy and stained burlap sack that stinks of rot and decay. Inside is a thick skeletal left hand covered in moldy, green-gray flesh. Each of the four fingers stands up and erect, and the thumb is tucked in close to the palm. Each of the four fingertips has a small black wick showing. It is a *hand of glory*.
8	A shabby, floppy purple cloak with two white feathers. It is a *poet's cloak*.
9	A small velvet sack containing 2d10 enchanted six-sided *chaos dice* (see **Appendix B: New Magic Items**).
10	A small sack appears with 6d6 tiny gemstones (diamond, emeralds, rubies, and sapphires), each worth 20 gp.
11	A hollowed-out ram's horn fashioned into a war horn. It is a *horn of battle clarity*.
12	A coal-black warhammer appears. It is *Cruuf'xk's Warhammer* (see **Appendix B: New Magic Items**).

Room 9: Contraption Factory

From the hallway outside, it is easy to hear the *ting-ting* of tiny hammers crafting deadly toys. Inside the room, it is dark and poorly lit. Working in the room are 10 Crueltide elves, each seated at a table with a pair of low-burning candles providing the lighting needed for their tasks. The room is old — ancient even — and the ceiling sags, a portion of the north wall has fallen in, and a corridor to the west has collapsed and is full of rubble.

The elderly **Crueltide elves** in this chamber seem as ancient and feeble as the room itself. None of them has the strength or stamina to battle the adventurers, but five new experimental contraptions are ready to defend their creators: the meka-men! Each **meka-man** stands seven feet tall and is made of iron. Their bodies are covered in filigree and fancy sculpting details, and they are painted in bright colors with rosy red cheeks and big eyes. Four of the meka-men wield weapons, while the other holds a wand.

Each geriatric Crueltide elf has only 1 hit point and no armor; they are easily slain. Anyone searching the room may roll 1d6: on a 1–4, they find broken and incomplete contraptions; on a 5–6, they find one contraption (roll on the **Crueltide Contraptions Table**).

Crueltide Elf (10) CR 1/2
XP 100
hp 9 (currently 1) (Appendix A: New Monsters, "Crueltide Elf")

No Gear

Meka-Man Soldier (4) CR 6
XP 2,400
hp 64 (Pathfinder Roleplaying Game Bestiary 3, "Clockwork Soldier")

Meka-Man Mage CR 9
XP 6,400
hp 102 (Pathfinder Roleplaying Game Bestiary 4, "Clockwork Mage")

Wand is Evocation

Room 10: Lost Souls

The tortured moans and cries of prisoners fill this room. A curtain of chains separates this room from a corridor to the north, and an open sarcophagus positioned above a bed of red-hot coals is along the south wall. Exhausted and defeated prisoners are shackled to the walls. Their torturers are a band of twisted people with horns, demonic grins, hooved feet, and stinger tails. One of them sees your crew of adventurers and says, "Oh look! Fresh meat!"

The thirteen demonic creatures are known as the **Naughty**. This room is where they torture their hapless victims. They place a prisoner into the sarcophagus and then fill it with candy canes. The coals under the sarcophagus are stoked until the candy canes melt. The Naughty then remove the candied golem and place it in **Room 11** for safekeeping. If rescued, the five prisoners can help the characters as hirelings fighting for their freedom, and if a character dies, a prisoner can serve as a replacement. The insanity and torture the **prisoners** endured has turned them all into barbarians.

Naughty (13) CR 3
XP 800
hp 26 (Tome of Horrors Complete, "Hoar Spirit")

Prisoner (5) CR 1/2
XP 200
hp 15 (Pathfinder Roleplaying Game NPC Codex, "Savage Mercenary")

No Gear

Room 11: Sweet Tomb

This circular chamber has a 25-foot-high domed ceiling and five niches evenly spaced around the northern hemisphere of the room. A large sarcophagus is within each niche. The lid of each sarcophagus is sculpted to resemble a giant candy-jellied bear, and each is painted a different color: blue, red, yellow, green, and purple. A two-foot-diameter red-and-white striped orb hangs from a short chain in the center of the domed ceiling. The orb spins slowly.

As the characters enter this chamber, the spinning orb begins to glow with an internal white light that pulses like a heartbeat. The orb returns to a dormant mode when no one is in the room. Each jelly-bear sarcophagus contains 2d3 + 1 **candied golems** that the Naughty created in **Room 10**. They are piled in the crypts like cordwood. Each candied golem is in a state of suspended animation; the key to their animation is slowly spinning on the ceiling.

The orb fires a bolt of lightning at two sarcophagi as it is able. When the lightning strikes, one of the candied golems inside each sarcophagus animates. The golems slide open their tombs and lumber out to attack.

The secret to this room is to destroy the **spinning orb**. Without it, the candied golems cannot be reanimated.

Candied Golem (10d3 + 5) CR 3
XP 800
hp 42 (Pathfinder Roleplaying Game Bestiary 4, "Golem, Wax")

Spinning Orb CR 1/2
XP 200
hp 6 (Appendix A: New Monsters, "Spinning Orb")

Room 12: Demonic Choir

The music heard throughout this candied crypt grows louder as you approach this chamber. As you enter, you discover a 13-piece demonic orchestra, but each humanoid musician is skinless, and their instruments are abominations constructed out of bones. Standing on the small stage is the choir, a quartet of demons singing in perfect harmony.

As noted in **Beginning the Adventure** above, remind the players about the music and the singing that echoes through this dungeon. The orchestra is impervious to harm. If a musician is slain, it just stands back up during the next combat round to continue playing its instrument. If its instrument is destroyed, it automatically knits back together so it can be played again. The musicians have no action other than playing music.

The four members of the choir are **erinyes**. At least one erinyes must continue singing to maintain control of the orchestra. If all four erinyes are destroyed, their grip on the orchestra is released. As soon as the last erinyes dies, the orchestra changes its tune and begins playing a melody that sounds like the opening theme music for the *Tales from the Crypt* television series. The new song also echoes throughout the Candy Crypt. The orchestra's musicians despise Orcus' Claws, so the new song bestows a +1-morale bonus to hit and to saving throws for the player characters while it is playing.

Erinye (4) CR 8
XP 4,800
hp 94 (Pathfinder Roleplaying Game Bestiary, "Devil, Erinye")

Area 13: Dangerous Hall

The floor and ceiling of this long hallway are painted a bright white. The walls are decorated with brightly painted frescos depicting the mighty Orcus' Claws visiting merry mayhem on hapless villagers.

A new fresco image is found every 10 feet along the hallway. Starting at **Room 1** (fresco 1 on table below) and running to **Room 18** (fresco 10), the images depicted along the hallway are:

Fresco	Description
1	Orcus' Claws driving his sleigh through a pale evening sky filled with black stars.
2	Orcus' Claws looking jolly as his reindeer are slaughtering and eating frightened villagers.
3	Orcus' Claws stuffing frightened children into his bulging sack.
4	Orcus' Claws relaxing and reclining in a comfy chair as he pulls a strip of meat off a bone with his teeth. The foot on the leg is still wearing a pink bunny slipper. Claws has a glass of milk in his other hand. (Trapped)
5	Orcus' Claws looking over his shoulder to smile and wink at the viewer as he warms his hands over a burning holiday tree with a restrained family tied to the trunk.
6	Orcus' Claws placing bloodstained weapons decorated in colorful ribbons and bows under the holiday tree. A severed hand lies nearby in a pool of bright red blood. (Trapped)
7	Orcus' Claws in full belly laugh as a trio of animated dolls with knives surround and menacingly close in on a frightened little girl.
8	Orcus' Claws placing a large candy cane into a stocking nailed to a fireplace mantel, but the stocking is already bulging and overstuffed with creepy crawling insects. A wet eyeball with a few inches of optical nerve sits on the mantel near the stocking. (Trapped)
9	Orcus' Claws walking back toward his sleigh. Two crying and defeated kids are slung over one shoulder, and he drags a third kid behind him by the hair.
10	Orcus' Claws and his sleigh of flying reindeer silhouetted against a full moon as a village burns below them.

The hallway is trapped at Frescos 4, 6, and 8:

Fresco No. 4 Trap: Anyone stepping in front of this fresco must make a Reflex saving throw or fall 10 feet into a 20-foot-by-20-foot room. Three **demonic reindeer** with glowing red eyes stalk the room and instantly attack anyone who falls into their den.

Fresco No. 4 Pit Trap   CR 1/2
XP 200
Type mechanical; **Perception** DC 20; **Disable Device** DC 20
Trigger location; **Reset** manual
Effect 10-ft.-deep pit (1d6 falling damage); DC 20 Reflex avoids; multiple targets (all targets in a 10-ft.-square area)

Demonic Reindeer (3)   CR 3
XP 800
hp 30 (Pathfinder Roleplaying Game Bestiary, "Hell Hound")

Fresco No. 6 Trap: A huge axe blade swings on a pendulum between the walls to strike at anyone stepping in front of this fresco. The frescos conceal the slit from which the pendulum swings. After the blade swings, dozens of poisoned needles rain down from the ceiling.

Swinging Axe Trap   CR 1
XP 400
Type mechanical; **Perception** DC 20; **Disable Device** DC 20
Trigger location; **Reset** manual
Effect Atk +10 melee (axe; 1d8 + 1/×3); multiple targets (all targets in a 10-ft. line)

Poison Needle Volley Trap   CR 2
XP 600
Type mechanical; **Perception** DC 20; **Disable Device** DC 20
Trigger location; **Reset** manual
Effect Poison needles (Atk +10 ranged, 1 plus poison [blue whinnis]); multiple targets (all targets in a 10-ft.-square area)

Blue Whinnis Poison
Type poison (injury); **Save** Fortitude DC 14; **Frequency** 1/round for 2 rounds; **Cure** 1 save
Initial Effect: 1 Con damage
Secondary Effect: Unconsciousness for 1d3 hours

Fresco No. 8 Trap: The 10-foot-by-10-foot section of floor in front of this fresco is thin and easily breaks away. Anyone stepping in front of this fresco sinks into a pit filled with insects. The pit is 30 feet deep, and it's filled nearly to the top with insects. Because of the insects' constant squirming, anyone caught in the pit begins to quickly sink and drown.

Characters must succeed on a DC 15 Swim check each round to "swim" through the insects and keep their head above the squirming mass. Failure results in sinking 10 ft. They can succeed on a check on the next round to claw their way back up. Once on the "surface," characters can climb out of the pit with a successful DC 15 Climb check.

Fresco No. 8 Pit Trap   CR 1/2
XP 200
Type mechanical; **Perception** DC 20; **Disable Device** DC 20
Trigger location; **Reset** manual
Effect 30-ft.-deep pit (1d6 falling damage plus centipede swarms); DC 20 Reflex avoids; multiple targets (all targets in a 10-ft.-square area)

Centipede Swarm (2)   CR 4
XP 1,200
hp 31 (Pathfinder Roleplaying Game Bestiary, "Centipede Swarm")

Room 14: Bittersweet Treats

This room is a beehive of activity. Raw candy ore is delivered on a series of conveyer belts. The ore is plucked from the belts, torn and crushed into smaller bits, and then mixed with other components to create pounds of tasty holiday treats. Four large tentacled monstrosities are hard at work in this candy factory; each of their tentacles is decorated in little silver bells that jangle as they work. If the legends are to be believed, before you is a quartet of jinglejells!

The **jinglejells** are focused on their work, and they attack the characters only if they are attacked first or if any character enters their zone. Each jinglejell works in a 20-foot-by-20-foot zone separated by a thick column. At the rear of each zone, a narrow passage leads to the conveyer belt from **Room 7**. Some of the ore is automatically scraped off the belt as it passes each location, making a slowly growing pile for jinglejells to use.

If the jinglejells are defeated, the characters discover stacks and stacks of boxed candied treats and the corpse of an unfortunate soul who lost his life to the jingle grells long ago.

Jinglejell (4)   CR 6
XP 2,400
hp 31 (Appendix A: New Monsters, "Jinglejell")

The corpse is that of Montague J. Sebastian, a famed astrologer, sage, and wizard who vanished many years ago. It seems that the characters have solved the riddle of his disappearance. Sebastian's corpse holds the following treasures: a *greater caster's shield*, a *magician's hat*, a *ring of counterspells*, a *robe of the archmagi (white)*, a *staff of power*, an ivory and mahogany *+1 light crossbow* with a dozen silver bolts, and his spellbook *artic call (with preparation ritual)*. Do note to your players that this is a full *Archmage's Vestments* Magic Item Set for the feats Collector's Boon and Improved Collector's Boon from *Pathfinder Player Companion: Chronicle of Legends*.

Room 15: Storage

> Life-sized wooden dolls fill this large chamber. None of the wooden dolls is painted or decorated; instead, they either have a light pine varnish or a darker oak, pecan, or maple stain. Some of the wooden dolls are more than six feet tall, while others are only three feet tall. Some are thin and svelte, while others are broad and heavy. None of the dolls appears to have a definitive gender, but some seem vaguely masculine, some appear more feminine, and a few are genderless. This room is so full of wooden dolls that it is impossible to move through it without pushing past and brushing up against two or more dolls with every step taken.

The wooden dolls are the remains of adventurers who attempted to plunder Orcus' Claws' Candy Crypt. The unfortunate adventurers were transformed into wooden dolls by the bite of a creature known as a **pheasatrice**. A secret coop of six pheasatrices is hidden in the southwest corner of the room. Once characters start moving through the room, the sound of the wooden dolls knocking against each other alerts the creatures that prey has entered their lair.

Pheasatrice (6)   CR 3
XP 800
hp 27 (Pathfinder Roleplaying Game Bestiary, "Cockatrice")

Petrification changes to wood instead of stone

The Puzzle: The east corridor leads to the office (**Room 16**), but a portcullis blocks the corridor. A manual wheel to lift the portcullis is in **Room 16**, but it cannot be seen or operated by anyone inside **Room 15**. Instead, the storage room has a magical puzzle lock that can raise the portcullis. The east corridor is gothic in design, with a peaked arch that is 12 feet high at the summit. Unique clay tiles outline the arch. The tile at the peak of the arch is embossed with a star-shaped ridge, and all the tiles that outline the rest of the archway have a gutter that flows down to a pair of small holes in the floor. Any liquid poured onto the star-embossed tile at the peak splits into two channels and flows down either side of the archway, where it eventually drains into the holes on the floor. Closer inspection of the star-embossed tile reveals the ridge has an egg-shaped background. The enchanted portcullis is impervious to magical and physical harm and cannot be lifted.
The Solution: The characters need to smash a pheasatrice egg against the star-embossed tile at the peak of the archway. The bloodied yolk then oozes down both sets of guttered tiles on either side of the archway and drains into the holes on the floor. Throwing an egg at the star-embossed tile requires a successful ranged attack against AC 19. One character could also lift another onto their shoulders to smash the egg against the tile by hand. When the egg cracks and the yolk spills down the gutters, each tile illuminates in a golden yellow light. Manually cracking two eggs into the drains at the base of the arch does not raise the portcullis.
Medium or larger characters must squeeze while in the room because of the multitude of wooden dolls, and the entire area is difficult terrain for all characters. The wall concealing the pheasatrices' coop has gaps in the bricks that the creatures can move through. Knocking down the wall of loosely stacked bricks exposes the coop. The six pheasatrices typically leave the coop one at a time to attack intruders, but if the wall concealing their coop is knocked down, all remaining pheasatrices attack. The coop contains 3d6 pheasatrice eggs, each worth 250 gp to an alchemist.

Room 16: The Office

> The large bloodstained stone altar in the center of the room is being used as a desk. Four torches on eight-foot-tall iron rods are positioned near the corners of the desk. A dour-looking human wearing expensive robes sits at the desk and scratches at a scroll with a quill in his hand.

A wheel that operates the portcullis in the corridor leading to the storage area (**Room 15**) is in the northwest corner of the room. The gentleman introduces himself as **Sir Ramasin Kalam**, a demi-knight, scribe, and oracle tasked with managing the daily operations of the Candy Crypt. In truth, Kalam is a rakshasa with a scimitar named *Hawkeye* (see **Appendix B: New Magic Items**). Kalam does not want to be disturbed. He refuses to help anyone who calls out to him from the portcullis, and he becomes terribly angry if anyone enters his room. While in his human guise, Kalam appears to have a great tiger tattoo across his chest and back. When he transforms into his true rakshasa form, the tattoo ripples, envelops his whole body, and he manifests as a ferocious tiger-man.

Sir Ramasin Kalam   CR 10
XP 9,600
hp 115 (Pathfinder Roleplaying Game Bestiary, "Rakshasa")

Replace *+1 kukri* with *Hawkeye*

If Kalam is destroyed and the desk searched, the characters discover a scroll titled, *Opening the Way through Gorgon Major* (see **side box**). The scroll details the ritual required to open a gateway for Nohell Claws to return to this plane of existence, as well as a separate ritual for closing and sealing the gate. The Gorgon Major gate can be closed only by using this scroll. In addition to the scroll, the adventurers discover a *luckstone* being used as a paperweight, a leather-bound book written by Sir Ramasin Kalam titled, *Eye of the Tiger: A Memoir* (it is a *tome of clear thought +1*), a *crystal ball* on a small bronze tripod, and a small chest with 3d10 + 20 gp and 2d12 small gems worth 30 gp each.

> ## Opening the Way through Gorgon Major (Scroll)
>
> This scroll contains the ritual needed to open or close the Gorgon Major gate. For the characters to use the scroll to close the gate, one character must maintain concentration (as if concentrating on a spell) for a total of five rounds (not necessarily consecutive) while reading from the scroll before Mr. Giggles does the same. In the event of a tie, Mr. Giggles wins. If the Gorgon Major gate is successfully opened, Nohell Claws steps through. See the Observatory (**Room 19**) for more details.

Area 17: The Void

> The hallway narrows to only five feet wide for a distance of 10 feet. The cobblestone floor is unchanged in the short stretch of hallway, but the walls and ceiling are dramatically different. The walls and ceiling are black as pitch, and they seem to rapidly vibrate with a subsonic hum. Your hairs rise into gooseflesh as you draw closer. Your gut tells you that something is very wrong with the walls in that part of the hallway, something otherworldly.

The disturbing portion of the hallway is a wound, an open scar to a plane of chaos that hungers for life and that literally attempts to grab anyone who passes through the narrow corridor. As the characters move through the narrow corridor, 1d3 + 1 arms and tentacles of various sizes and shapes reach from the void to grab each of them. They act on Initiative 20, losing ties. Each appendage makes an attack at +7 to hit CMD. On a success, the target is grappled (CMD 14 + 2 for each appendage above one that has grappled the target. The first round an appendage starts its turn with a creature grappled, that creature is pulled halfway into the void. The second round the appendage start its turn with the same creature grappled, that creature is pulled through the wall and lost forever. A creature that is not grappled may attempt a DC 14 (+2 per additional appendage) Strength check to pull a grappled creature free of the appendages.

Room 18: The Throne Room

> This room is enormous, with a ceiling that is 30 feet high. Three huge 15-foot-diameter chandeliers are evenly spaced down the length of the room, each casting a sickly yellow light into every corner of the room. A huge line of seemingly mindless people is queued in a zig-zag pattern that runs the full length of the room. The procession begins in a niche in the northwest corner of the room, where an open dimensional door allows the people to slowly shuffle through. The line ends at the southern end of the room, where jolly ol' Orcus' Claws sits upon a throne of bones. The bones are festively painted red, white, and green.

The belly laugh of **Orcus' Claws** (see **Appendix A: New Creatures**) is more of a "Har-har-harrr" than a "Ho-ho-hooo!" Claws has delegated the task of summoning his beloved Nohell Claws to his able astrologer, Mr. Giggles, which allows Claws the time to convert more damned souls into his legion of the Naughty. It takes three combat rounds of Claws whispering into the ear of a soulless wretch to transform it into one of the Naughty. Claws cannot belly laugh and whisper to the soulless at the

same time. When the characters enter the room, Claws has already created four of the **Naughty**. Six **Crueltide elves** and 10 **brownie bites** manage the line of soulless wretches. The wretches only have 1 hit point each and AC 10. They feel no pain and take no interest in anything or anyone around them.

The portal from which the procession of soulless wretches emerge leads to a level deep within the Abyss. If the characters choose to escape the Candy Crypt by traveling to the Abyss, then you should close the curtains on this adventure and prepare something for them to explore in the Abyss.

Brownie Bite (10) CR 1
XP 400
hp 4 (Pathfinder Roleplaying Game Bestiary, "Brownie")

Change **Alignment** to NE

Crueltide Elf (6)   CR 1
XP 400
hp 9 (Appendix A: New Monsters, "Crueltide Elf")

Naughty (4)   CR 3
XP 800
hp 26 (Tome of Horrors Complete, "Hoar Spirit")

Orcus' Claws   CR 10
XP 9,600
hp 137 (Appendix A: New Monsters, "Orcus' Claws")

If he senses his end is near, Orcus' Claws teleports away in a cloud of fire and brimstone to a secret lair deep within the Abyss to recuperate. If his throne is searched, the characters discover a large chest hidden in a secret compartment under the seat. The chest is trapped and releases a cloud of poisonous gas in a 10-foot radius unless the trap is successfully disarmed.

Throne Gas Trap   CR 8
XP 4,800
Type mechanical; **Perception** DC 25; **Disable Device** DC 20
Trigger location; **Reset** repair
Effect poison gas (insanity mist); never miss; onset delay (1 round); multiple targets (all targets in a 10-ft. radius)

Insanity Mist   CR 8
XP 4800
Type poison (inhaled); **Save** Fortitude DC 15; **Frequency** 1/round for 6 rounds; **Cure** 1 save
Effect 1d3 Wis damage

The chest contains 4d6 x 50 gp, 3d12 large gems worth 125 gp each, a black silk sack containing a *robe of eyes*, a pan flute made from human bones (*pipes of the sewers*), and a stone earth elemental figurine set on a cheap tinsel ring (a *ring of elemental command [earth]*).

ROOM 19: THE OBSERVATORY

This large room has a domed ceiling enchanted to display a dark sky full of stars in motion. The stars make up the amazing constellation of Gorgon Major as it rises above a vortex gateway of swirling energy on the east wall. The silhouette of a bat-winged woman with long flowing hair is fighting her way through the vortex to enter this chamber. Standing before the vortex is a dwarf with fluffy pink hair and a beard, and he wears a robe covered in gumdrops. The dwarf is raising his arms toward the vortex and chanting at the portal. As you enter the room, a host of demonic minions in the room turn to face you!

A lot is happening in this room, so take careful note of all the moving parts. The four main aspects of this room are:
1) Mr. Giggles needs to maintain concentration for five total rounds to finish opening the Gorgon Major gate;
2) A character needs to maintain concentration for five total while reading from the scroll to permanently close the Gorgon Major gate;
3) The horde of demonic minions is ready to battle the characters;
4) Nohell Claws might enter the room and engage the characters.
Mr. Giggles is not a true dwarf; he is actually a dwarf-like demon known as a faerhle. Each round, if Mr. Giggles attempts to maintain concentration on his spell to open the portal.

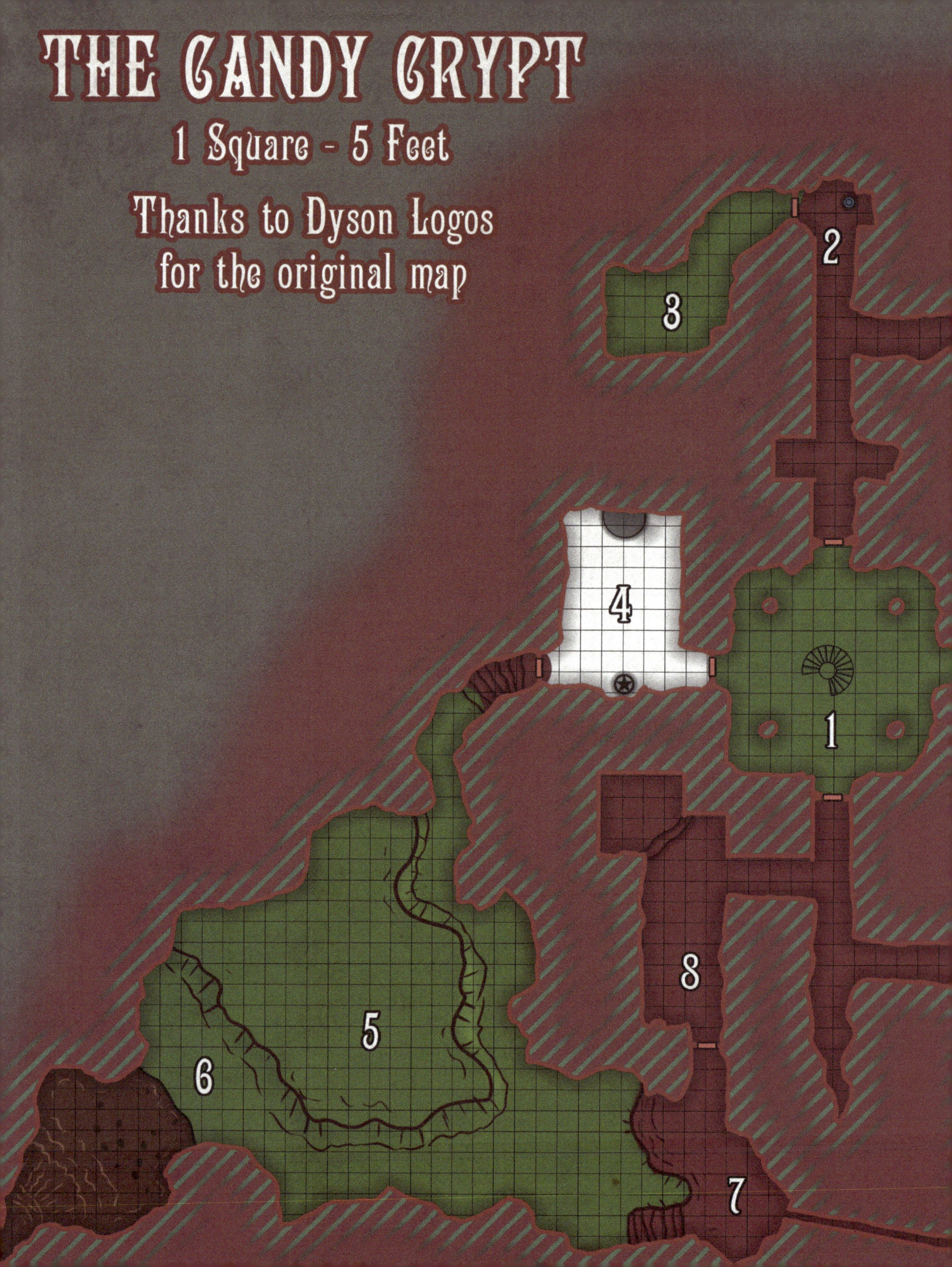

THE CANDY CRYPT

1 Square - 5 Feet

Thanks to Dyson Logos
for the original map

9
10
11
12
13
14
15
16
17
18
19

A character reading from the *Opening the Way through Gorgon Major* scroll (see sidebox in the Office [**Room 16**]) may also attempt to maintain concentration to close the Gorgon Major gate.

The demonic minions in the room are **alu-demons** and, as luck would have it, there are the same number of alu-demons as there are characters.

Nohell Claws is a unique succubus demon. She is ample and curvy and the bride of Orcus' Claws. She has been trapped in a realm beyond the stars for a millennium. Finally, the stars are right, and a way can be opened for her return. Nohell can sense the characters fighting against her return, and it enrages her. If she successfully escapes her exile, she exacts her wrath upon the characters.

Alu-Demon (# of characters)   **CR 5**
XP 1,600
hp 45 (Tome of Horrors Complete, "Demon, Alu-")

Mr. Giggles   **CR 6**
XP 2,400
hp 68 (Appendix A: New Monsters, "Demon, Faerhle")

Nohell Claws   **CR 8**
XP 4,800
hp 100 (Appendix A: New Monsters, "Nohell Claws")

FINAL CONFLICT?

Ideally, the conflict in the Observatory (**Room 19**) is the conclusion of this dungeon delve. Assuming the characters defeat Mr. Giggles and prevent Nohell Claws from entering this realm (or if she does enter and they defeat her), then the looming threat in this adventure has been resolved and you can "fade to black" with the players having had a satisfying end to the game. However, it is also likely that the characters did not fully explore the Candy Crypt before the finale occurred. So what should you do if your players want to continue exploring this sugar and spice hellscape?

The denizens of the Candy Crypt are anxiously awaiting the coming of Nohell Claws, and they sense if she is repelled or defeated. In that case, if the orchestra is still under the thumb of the choir of erinyes, then the music changes in pitch and tone to something more somber and dire. This new melody of melancholy grants all creatures native to the Candy Crypt a +2-morale bonus to hit and damage rolls. The foul creatures that dwell within the Candy Crypt have no reason to retreat or flee from the invasive adventurers.

New monsters found in this merry adventure are listed below.

BUBBLEGUM SPHERE   CR 2

XP 600
N Medium aberration
Init +1; **Senses** darkvision 60 ft.; Perception +5
AC 13, touch 11, flat-footed 12 (+1 Dex, +2 natural)
hp 20 (3d8+6)
Fort +3, **Ref** +2, **Will** +3
Defensive Abilities all-around vision, amorphous; **Immune** electricity, fire
Speed fly 20 ft. (good)
Melee slam +5 (1d6 + 4 plus grab)
Special Attacks swallow whole (1d6 + 4, AC 11, 2 hp)
Str 16, **Dex** 13, **Con** 14, **Int** 3, **Wis** 10, **Cha** 7
Base Atk +2; **CMB** +5 (+13 grapple); **CMD** 16 (20 vs. grapple, can't be tripped)
Feats Flyby Attack, Power Attack
Skills Fly +9, Perception +5
SQ adhesive
Special Abilities
Adhesive (DC 13) (Ex) A bubblegum sphere exudes a thick tar-like substance that acts as a powerful adhesive, holding fast any creatures or items touching it unless they succeed on a Strength check.
Swallow Whole (1d6 + 4, AC 11, 2 HP) (Ex) You can swallow creatures of up to medium size whole.

Bubblegum spheres are a spherical mass of gelatinous polymer, with an outer surface that is gummy and sticky. Contrary to popular belief, they are not hollow on the inside.

CRUELTIDE ELF   CR 1

XP 400
CE Small humanoid (goblinoid)
Init +1; **Senses** Perception -1
AC 12, touch 12, flat-footed 11 (+1 Dex, +1 size)
hp 9 (2d8)
Fort +0, **Ref** +4, **Will** -1
Speed 30 ft.
Melee Fire Poker +3 (1d6 - 2)
Special Attack Crueltide Contraptions - Crueltide elves carry a small pouch that contains 1d2 Crueltide contraptions (see chart)
Str 6, **Dex** 12, **Con** 10, **Int** 12, **Wis** 8, **Cha** 10
Base Atk +1; **CMB** -2; **CMD** 8
Feats Weapon Finesse, Catch Off-Guard
Skills Craft (Contraptions) +6, Stealth +6, Climb +3
Languages Common, Goblin

These strange goblinoid beasts have been corrupted by the influences of Orcus and the dark forces of winter. They have wicked, inhuman grins filled with needle-like teeth, sallow orange skin, and unusually pointed ears. They wield weapons of crudely crafted iron that leave jagged and painful wounds and laugh and cackle as they fight. They wear ridiculous red-and-green motley and often accentuate their outfits with curled-toe shoes. Many wear bells atop their pointed caps.

Despite their name, Crueltide elves are not true elves. They simply call themselves such for their own twisted enjoyment. They are instead a strange sub-race of goblins, though they are quite skilled at mechanical engineering — especially when it comes to designing deadly toys. Each Crueltide elf carries a bag containing several Crueltide contraptions — wicked and deadly toys — that they gleefully use in battle. The table below lists various Crueltide contraptions, but you are free to invent more for the wicked little goblins to use.

CRUELTIDE CONTRAPTIONS

Crueltide elves carry a small pouch that contains Crueltide contraptions:

CRUELTIDE CONTRAPTIONS

1d12	Contraption
1	**Easy Burn Oven**: This small metal box generates enormous heat when cooking cakes no larger than a gold piece. One round after being activated, the Easy Burn Oven flies open in a gout of fire and fills a 20 foot area around it with thick, vision-obstructing smoke. Ranged attacks in this area suffer a –4 penalty, and all spellcasting attempts in the thick smoke have a 20% chance of failure as everyone in the smoke coughs and sputters. The smoke disperses after 1d4 rounds. This can only be activated again once the smoke has dispersed.
2	**Mini-Rocket Cart**: These tiny metal and wooden carts carry a small but deadly payload of oil and fire. They have a wind-up key on the side. After being wound up (which takes one full round), the Mini-Rocket Cart travels 30ft forward in whatever direction it has been pointed and explodes, doing 1d8 points of damage to anyone within 10ft of the blast (DC 12 Reflex save for half damage).
3	**Rider Red's Bee-Bee Crossbow**: A child-sized hand crossbow with a strange collection of gears, flywheels, and pullies, this small weapon fires a projectile at dangerous velocity. It fires standard crossbow bolts but inflicts 1d12 points of damage with a range of 20ft. However, it is notoriously inaccurate, and all attacks made with the Rider Red's Bee-Bee Crossbow are done at a –4 penalty. If the attacker rolls a natural 1 on their attack, the bolt ricochets and hits the operator in the eye, causing the eye to be lost until *regeneration* can be applied. The crossbow typically comes with five bolts.
4	**Snow-Wrapped Caltrop**: These are simply large snowballs with nasty, rusted caltrops at their center. They can be thrown up to 30ft and still remain effective. They inflict 1d4 + 1 points of damage upon a successful attack. After the fist-sized caltrop is removed, the ensuing wound bleeds for another 1d2 points of damage.
5	**Wind-up Toy Soldier**: This tiny tin militia man has a large wind-up key that requires one full round to crank. On the following round, the soldier marches forward 10 feet and opens fire with its adorable but deadly crossbow on the nearest target. It can fire once each round at +2 to hit for 1d6 damage for three rounds before it runs out of ammunition and falls dormant. The soldier's ammunition reloads in one day when it can be wound up and used again.
6	**Wendy Wetsie Doll**: This creepy, glass-eyed porcelain doll whines loudly for one round after a small button on her back is pressed. On the following round, she falls silent and an impossibly large pool of slick, stinking yellow liquid spews forth from the doll, making a 20ft area around Wendy Wetsie extraordinarily slick and difficult to traverse. Anyone attempting to cross the soiled area must make a DC 12 Reflex saving throw or fall prone. Those moving at half speed suffer no penalty, while characters moving at regular speed or running suffer a –2 or –4 penalty, respectively.

1d12	Contraption
7	**Cracker-Jax**: This toy consists of a ball and 2d4 caltrops. The small red rubber ball has two stark-white stars painted on the sides and is packed with explosive powder and metal shards. A small fuse sticks out of the ball. The Crueltide elf lights the fuse and bounces the ball at a point of its choosing up to 20 feet away. The ball explodes and all creatures within 10 feet of the point must make a DC 15 Reflex saving throw, taking 1d8 force damage on a failure or half as much on a success. The caltrops are dropped on the floor to protect the elf; any creature that ends its turn within five feet of the elf must make a DC 10 Reflex saving throw to avoid the caltrops. On a failed save, the creature takes 1d4 piercing damage.
8	**Dolly Doo-Whip**: This cute doll has long sweeping hair. The Crueltide elf grabs the doll and begins to swing her around vigorously. With each swing, the doll's hair gets longer, longer, and longer. One round after drawing the doll, the doll's hair turns into a 15-foot-long whip with barbs on the end. With a successful melee attack, the hair-whip inflicts 1d6 + 1 piercing damage.
9	**Rolling Blades**: These are a pair of deadly wheeled shoes covered in razor-sharp blades. The Crueltide elf may don the skates with a swift action. The first time the elf moves within five feet of a creature on the elf's turn while wearing these skates, the creature must succeed on a DC 14 Reflex saving throw or take 1d4 slashing damage. The elf is immune to opportunity attacks while wearing these skates.
10	**Stick Horse**: This toy is a three-foot-long stick with a jet-black horse head on one end. The toy horse head is that of a nightmare, with bright red eyes and a mane. Up to three times per day, the elf can quickly double-tap the stick on the floor to cause the nightmare stick horse to shoot fire from its eyes. The elf makes a ranged touch attack against a target within 20 feet. The fire inflicts 1d6 fire damage on a hit.
11	**Tribal Drum**: This musical instrument stands two feet tall and has a 10-inch-diameter drumhead. The elf tucks the drum under one arm and begins striking it with the other hand. The drum produces a sound that is hypnotic to all non-evil creatures. Creatures who hear the enchanted music must succeed on a DC 14 Will saving throw or be affected as if by a *charm person* spell.
12	**Voodoo Dolly**: This soft cloth dolly has nondescript features and a clay head. If the Crueltide elf makes a successful melee attack against an injured foe, the dolly soaks up some of the foe's blood. The dolly's clay head then transforms into the likeness of the foe whose blood it absorbed, cementing the bond between the voodoo dolly and the target. Three times per day, the Crueltide elf can stab the voodoo dolly with a needle to inflict 1d6 piercing damage to the bonded victim. The elf can instead hold the voodoo dolly over an open flame to immediately inflict 4d6 fire damage to the bonded target but this destroys the dolly.

Demon, Faerhle
CR 6

XP 2,400
CE Medium outsider (chaotic, demon, evil)
Init +2; **Senses** darkvision 120 ft.; Perception +12
AC 20, touch 12, flat-footed 18 (+8 armor, +2 Dex)
hp 68 (8d10+24)
Fort +9, **Ref** +4, **Will** +7; +2 vs. poison, spells, and spell-like abilities
DR 5/magic; **Immune** electricity, poison; **Resist** acid 10, cold 10, fire 10; SR 16
Weaknesses light sensitivity
Speed 20 ft.
Melee *+1 frost heavy flail* +13/+8 (1d10 + 5/17-20 plus 1d6 cold)
Special Attacks cotton candy beard
Str 16, **Dex** 15, **Con** 16, **Int** 13, **Wis** 13, **Cha** 14
Base Atk +8; **CMB** +11; **CMD** 23 (27 vs. bull rush and trip)
Feats Improved Critical (heavy flail), Power Attack, Weapon Evoker Mastery, Weapon Focus (heavy flail)
Skills Acrobatics +0 (-4 to jump), Knowledge (arcana) +12, Knowledge (planes) +12, Knowledge (religion) +12, Perception +12, Sense Motive +12, Spellcraft +12, Use Magic Device +13
Languages Abyssal, Common, Dwarven
SQ dwarf blood
Other Gear icelink chainmail, *+1 frost heavy flail*
Special Abilities
Cotton Candy Beard (1/1d4 rounds, DC 17) (Su) The faerhle shoots of a gob of its cotton-candy-like beard at a target within 30 feet. The target must succeed on a Fortitude saving throw or become entangled. While entangled, it is anchored and takes 1d6 acid damage at the beginning of each of its turns.
Weapon Evoker Mastery As a swift action, weapon dealing extra elemental damage adds +1d4 of same energy type.

Faerhle are unique demons that bear a strong resemblance to dwarves. Faerhles have three fingers on each hand, and their large beards are made up of a fluffy, sticky substance that grows in a variety of bright colors. A faerhle's beard is very much like cotton candy. Many faerhle arm themselves with flails or other heavy two-handed weapons.

Demon, Kringkuk
CR 4

XP 1,200
CE Small outsider (chaotic, demon, evil)
Init +7; **Senses** darkvision 120 ft.; Perception +11
AC 16, touch 14, flat-footed 13 (+3 Dex, +2 natural, +1 size)
hp 38 (5d10+10)
Fort +3, **Ref** +7, **Will** +7
Immune cold, electricity, poison; **Resist** acid 10, fire 10
Speed 20 ft., fly 40 ft. (average)
Melee bite +7 (1d6+1), 2 talons +7 (1d6+1)
Spell-Like Abilities (CL 5th; concentration +6)
  3/day—*web* (DC 13)
Str 13, **Dex** 16, **Con** 15, **Int** 10, **Wis** 16, **Cha** 13
Base Atk +5; **CMB** +5; **CMD** 18
Feats Flyby Attack, Improved Initiative, Power Attack
Skills Acrobatics +3 (-1 to jump), Fly +13, Knowledge (planes) +8, Perception +11, Profession (miner) +11, Sense Motive +11, Stealth +15

Kringkuks are a rare first-category arctic demon. They are snow white in color with an owl's torso and wings. Their large round head has six black, spider-like compound eyes and a tarantula's mandible. The demon has four pairs of insectoid legs that are covered in white fur instead of black chiton. Their two pairs of forelegs serve as the demon's arms, while the two rear pairs are the demon's legs.

Gingersnap Man
CR 1/2

XP 200
N Tiny construct
Init +2; **Senses** darkvision 60 ft., low-light vision; Perception +0
AC 14, touch 14, flat-footed 12 (+2 Dex, +2 size)
hp 6 (1d10)
Fort +0, **Ref** +2, **Will** +0
Immune construct traits, fire
Weaknesses vulnerability to water
Speed 40 ft.
Melee dagger +0 / +0 (1d2 - 1/19-20)
Space 2½ ft.; **Reach** 0 ft.
Str 8, **Dex** 15, **Con** —, **Int** —, **Wis** 10, **Cha** 3
Base Atk +1; **CMB** +1; **CMD** 10
Feats Two-weapon Fighting
Skills Acrobatics +2 (+6 to jump)
SQ candy curse
Other Gear candy cane dagger (2)
Special Abilities
Candy Curse (DC 13) (Su) Gingersnap men can be eaten but doing so could cost a creature its life. A creature that eats a gingersnap man is healed for 1d3 hit points but must make a Fortitude saving throw. The DC is equal to 13 minus the number of hit points recovered. On a failed save, the creature gains a candy curse:

Candy Curses

1d6	Candy Curse
1	The character's hair transforms into red and white taffy that smells like strawberries.
2	Shards of candy canes sprout from the character's shoulders, elbows, and knees.
3	Hot fudge oozes from the victim's eyes, ears, and nose, but it does not inhibit their ability to see, hear, or smell.
4	The character's flesh turns into soft cookie dough and has a warm and inviting smell. Chunks of the victim's flesh can be eaten, and the smell has an 80% chance of attracting wandering monsters.
5	The character's flesh secretes a sticky, sugary resin that makes it difficult for the victim to let go of items. The character must make a DC 18 Reflex saving throw to let go of weapons, doors, tankards of mead, or anything else. A DC 20 Strength check is also required to pull a weapon free if it is used to strike the character.
6	The character begins vomiting chocolate for 2d3 rounds. A character cannot take any other actions once it begins vomiting.

Candy curses can be cured with *remove curse*. If a creature gains four or more active candy curses at the same time, it dies from candy overload. When rolling for a new candy curse, reroll if the victim is already afflicted by that specific curse.

Gingersnap men stand 2–1/2 feet tall and are only six inches thick. They emerge from the hellfire oven already decorated with icing that defines their face and clothing. When a gingersnap man dies, it bleeds icing.

Jinglejell
CR 6

XP 2,400
Unique Frostfallen Giant Jellyfish
NE Large undead (cold)
Init +2; **Senses** lifesense; Perception +0
AC 15, touch 11, flat-footed 13 (+2 Dex, +4 natural, -1 size)
hp 31 (9d8-9)
Fort +1, **Ref** +5, **Will** +6
DR 5/bludgeoning; **Immune** cold, undead traits
Weaknesses vulnerability to fire
Speed fly 20 ft. (clumsy)
Melee slam +10 (2d6 + 5 plus 2d6 cold), 4 tentacles +10 (1d6 + 5 plus 2d6 cold)
Space 10 ft.; **Reach** 15 ft.
Special Attacks cold body, jingle bells
Str 20, **Dex** 15, **Con** —, **Int** —, **Wis** 10, **Cha** 7
Base Atk +6; **CMB** +12; **CMD** 24 (can't be tripped)
Feats Toughness
Skills Fly +0
Special Abilities
Cold Body (2d6) A frostfallen creature's body generates intense cold, dealing an amount of cold damage with its touch determined by its Hit Dice. Creatures attacking a frostfallen creature with unarmed strikes or natural weapons take this same cold damage each time one of their attacks hits.
Jingle Bells (DC 12) The jinglejell has 4 tentacles, each of which is decorated in silver bells that lend a rhythmic and musical quality to their movements. Anyone within 20 feet who listens to their jingling bells when the jinglejell takes a full attack action must succeed on a Will saving throw or be fascinated for 1 round.

Nohell Claws
CR 8

XP 4,800
CE Medium outsider (chaotic, cold, demon, elemental, evil, water)
Init +2; **Senses** darkvision 60 ft., detect good; Perception +21
Aura cold (2d6, 10 ft., DC 21)
AC 19, touch 12, flat-footed 17 (+2 Dex, +7 natural)
hp 100 (8d10+56)
Fort +9, **Ref** +8, **Will** +10
DR 10/good or cold iron; **Immune** bleed, cold, critical hits, electricity, flanking, paralysis, poison, precision damage, sleep, stunning; **Resist** acid 10; **SR** 18
Weaknesses vulnerability to fire
Speed 30 ft., fly 50 ft. (average); icewalking
Melee 2 claws +10 (1d6 + 1 plus 1d6 cold and paralysis)
Special Attacks energy drain (1 level, DC 22), exude ice, ice mastery, icy touch (1d6 cold and paralysis, DC 21), profane gift
Spell-Like Abilities (CL 12th; concentration +20)
Constant—*detect good, tongues*
At will—*charm monster* (DC 22), *detect thoughts* (DC 20), *ethereal jaunt* (self plus 50 lbs. of objects only), *greater teleport* (self plus 50 lbs. of objects only), *suggestion* (DC 21), *vampiric touch*
1/day—*dominate person* (DC 23), *summon* (level 3, 1 babau 50%)
Str 13, **Dex** 15, **Con** 24, **Int** 18, **Wis** 14, **Cha** 27
Base Atk +8; **CMB** +10; **CMD** 21
Feats Agile Maneuvers, Combat Reflexes, Iron Will, Weapon Finesse
Skills Acrobatics +7, Bluff +27, Diplomacy +19, Disguise +19, Escape Artist +10, Fly +13, Intimidate +16, Knowledge (local) +15, Perception +21, Sense Motive +13, Stealth +13; **Racial Modifiers** +5 Acrobatics, +8 Bluff, +8 Perception
Languages Abyssal, Aquan, Auran, Celestial, Common, Draconic; telepathy 100 ft., *tongues*
SQ change shape (small/medium humanoid; alter self), icy body
Special Abilities
Cold Aura (2d6, 10 ft., DC 21) (Ex) Those within range take 2d6 cold damage per round.
Exude Ice (At will) (Su) Exude 20-ft spread of slippery ice as a full-round action.
Ice Mastery (Ex) Gain +1 morale bonus on attack and damage if foe is touching ice.
Icewalking (Ex) Climb and move on icy surfaces without penalty & no Acrobatics checks to run or charge on ice.
Icy Body (Ex) Touching icy creature deals 1d6 cold damage.
Icy Touch (1d6 cold and paralysis, DC 21) (Ex) Natural attacks and metallic weapons deal 1d6 cold damage and may paralyze foes.
Profane Gift (1/day) (Su) Full round action to give humanoid +2 to an attribute, telepathic link. Can withdraw for 2d6 Cha drain.

Orcus' Claws
CR 10

XP 9,600
CE Large outsider (chaotic, demon, evil)
Init -1; **Senses** darkvision 60 ft.; Perception +17
AC 20, touch 8, flat-footed 20 (-1 Dex, +12 natural, -1 size)
hp 137 (13d10+65)
Fort +12, **Ref** +3, **Will** +9
DR 10/magic and silver; **Immune** cold, electricity, poison; **Resist** acid 10, fire 10; **SR** 20
Speed 30 ft., fly 30 ft. (poor)
Melee 2 claws +20 (1d6+7/19-20), sting +19 (1d4+7)
Space 10 ft.; **Reach** 10 ft.
Special Attacks deadly dance, flaming lump of coal, frozen poison
Spell-Like Abilities (CL 13th; concentration +17)
1/day—*plane shift* (self only)
Str 24, **Dex** 8, **Con** 18, **Int** 16, **Wis** 12, **Cha** 18
Base Atk +13; **CMB** +21; **CMD** 30
Feats Cleave, Cleaving Finish, Improved Critical (claw), Power Attack, Smiting Reversal, Toughness, Weapon Focus (claw)
Skills Bluff +20, Craft (traps) +19, Fly +9, Knowledge (planes) +19, Knowledge (religion) +19, Perception +17, Perform (dance) +20, Perform (sing) +20, Sense Motive +17
Languages Abyssal, Celestial, Common, Draconic; telepathy 100 ft.
SQ belly laugh
Special Abilities
Belly Laugh (1/1d4 rounds) (Su) All of Orcus' Claws allies within 60 feet of him that can hear him gain the benefit of *heroism* until the end of Orcus' Claws next turn.
Deadly Dance (1/minute, DC 20) (Su) Orcus' Claws cries out in a twisted singsong voice, "Bloody Solstice to all, and to all a great blight!" and dances. All targets within 120ft who hear his words must make a Will saving throw or be confused for 1d6 rounds.
Flaming Lump of Coal (1/1d4 rounds, DC 20) (Su) Orcus' Claws reaches into his sack and pulls out a flaming lump of coal, throwing it as the spell *fireball*.
Frozen Poison (DC 20) (Ex) Sting – injury; save Fort DC 20, frequency 1/round for 6 rounds, effect 1d4 Dex damage, cure 1 save
Smiting Reversal (+4 Atk, +13 dmg, 3/day) 3/day, AoO against enemy attempting to smite you, +4 to hit, +13 to damage.

As originally told in ***How Orcus Stole Christmas!*** by **Frog God Games**, this jolly aspect of the Demon Prince Orcus was crafted in the deepest pits of the Abyss by taking a single shaving from one of the Prince of the Undead's claws and freezing it in the coldest part of the Under Realms while enchanting it with vile magic. The creature that spewed forth, known as Orcus' Claws, is but a fragment of its progenitor's essence, yet it continues to grow ever stronger. Orcus' Claws is a corpulent beast standing seven feet tall and wearing a bloody mantle and stocking cap.

Spinning Orb
CR 1/2

XP 200
N Tiny construct
Init +2; **Senses** blindsight 60 ft., darkvision 60 ft., low-light vision; Perception +2
AC 16, touch 14, flat-footed 14 (+2 Dex, +2 natural, +2 size)
hp 6 (1d10)
Fort +0, **Ref** +2, **Will** +2
Defensive Abilities electric discharge; **Immune** construct traits, electricity
Speed 0 ft.
Space 2½ ft.; **Reach** 0 ft.
Special Attacks death burst
Str 2, **Dex** 15, **Con** —, **Int** —, **Wis** 14, **Cha** 3
Base Atk +1; **CMB** +1; **CMD** 7 (can't be tripped)
SQ spark of life
Special Abilities
Death Burst (DC 12) (Ex) The Spinning Orb explodes when it drops to 0 hit points. Each creature within 30 feet of it must make a Reflex saving throw, taking 2d6 electricity damage on a failure or half as much on a success.
Electric Discharge (DC 12) (Ex) When the spinning orb is hit by an attack, it sends a retributive lightning bolt at its attacker. The target must make a Reflex saving throw, taking 2d6 electricity damage on a failure or half as much on a success.
Spark of Life (1/1d4 rounds) (Su) The spinning orb fires a bolt of lightning at two sarcophagi. When the lightning strikes, one of the candied golems inside each sarcophagus animates. The golems slide open their tombs and lumber out to attack.

Appendix B: New Magic Items

New magic items found in this adventure are described below.

Chaos Dice (Minor Artifact)

Aura strong transmutation; **Slot** none; **CL** 20th; **Weight** —
A small velvet sack contains 2d10 of these enchanted six-sided dice that radiate warmth and have a soft green glow. You may only roll once per day, but you can roll any number of the six-sided dice simultaneously. For each die, consult the table below. After a die is rolled, that die dissolves into smoke and is lost forever.

1d6	Effect
1	Take 1d3 Con damage
2	Reduce maximum hit points by 1d6 for 24 hours
3	1d3 gemstones worth 80 gp each appear in your pocket
4	Gain a +1-inherent bonus to Strength for 24 hours
5	A single black rose appears; touching it grants you an amount of XP equal to an encounter with CR equal to you level, but the rose then withers and dies
6	Gain 1d6 hit points permanently, to a maximum of the maximum possible hit point total for your character

Cruuf'xk's Warhammer (Minor Artifact)

Aura strong necromancy; **Slot** none; **CL** 20th; **Weight** 5 lbs.
Alignment CE **Int** 16 **Wis** 14 **Cha** 20 **Ego** 14
Languages Abyssal, Common, Draconic, Infernal, telepathy
This intelligent *+2 warhammer* made of onyx contains the soul of Cruuf'xk, a demon of lies and temptations. Cruuf'xk's influence is strong; it telepathically whispers lies to you. It tells you that your so-called friends neither respect nor admire you. Your only true friend is Cruuf'xk, for you are bonded by blood and battle.
Three times per day as a free action when you hit with this weapon, you may call upon Cruuf'xk to inflict an additional 2d6 negative energy damage to your target.
The first time you use the warhammer in any combat, you must make a DC 14 Will saving throw. On a failed save, you submit to the corrupt and morally abhorrent suggestions made by Cruuf'xk for ten minutes. These might include attacking friends, stealing a sacred object, or looting money from children. The warhammer's depths of depravity know no bounds.

Frost Fang

Aura moderate evocation; **Slot** none; **CL** 11th; **Weight** 1 lb.; **Price** 36,002 gp
Alignment LG **Int** 18 **Wis** 10 **Cha** 14 **Ego** 12
Languages Aquan, Celestial, Common, Draconic, High Boros, telepathy
This *+1 frost dagger* was forged during the Age of Darkness by a master Hyperborean blacksmith. The dagger glows with a frosty blue light, and ice crystals form along the edge of the blade. While wielding *Frost Fang* you are immune to cold damage. In addition, you may cast *snowball* from the dagger up to three times per day.
Feats Craft Magical Arms and Armor, *chill metal* or *ice storm*, *resist energy*, *snowball*; **Cost** 18,001 gp

Hawkeye

Aura faint transmutation; **Slot** none; **CL** 9th; **Weight** 4 lbs.; **Price** 32,315 gp
Ramasin Kalam forged this *+3 training scimitar* when he completed his final quest to achieve his demi-knighthood. The curved blade was named *Hawkeye* for its ability to reflexively deflect incoming arrows and crossbow bolts. While wielding this weapon, you gain the benefit of the Deflect Arrows feat.
Feats Craft Magical Arms and Armor, *magic weapon*; **Cost** 16,315 gp

Ice Storm Sapphire (Minor Artifact)

Aura strong evocation; **Slot** none; **CL** 20th; **Weight** —
This large azure jewel glows with an inner white light. You can use the gem to cast *ice storm* a number of times per day that depends on the season. Damage also varies based on the season. You must make a successful DC 20 Fortitude saving throw when using the gem or take 1d6 cold damage.

Season	Number of Uses	Ice Storm Damage
Winter	3	3d6 bludgeoning and 6d6 cold damage in 40-foot-radius
Spring	2	3d6 bludgeoning and 4d6 cold damage in 30-foot-radius
Summer	1	2d6 bludgeoning and 4d6 cold damage in 20-foot-radius
Autumn	2	3d6 bludgeoning and 4d6 cold damage in 30-foot-radius

Magic Items for How Orcus Stole Christmas

Due to a printing error, the following items weren't included in the *Pathfinder* version of *How Orcus Stole Christmas*. To correct this, I am including them here.

Cane of Winter's Shepherd

Aura faint conjuration; **CL** 5th; **Price** 19,050 gp; **Weight** 4 lbs.
This long white shepherd's crook is bound in a band of red and functions as a *+1 staff* though its bearer gains several additional benefits. First, their breath is always minty fresh, and they can cast *purify food and drink* and *neutralize poison* three times per day. Not only is the food or beverage made perfectly edible, but they also gain a slight mint flavoring.
Feats Craft Magic Arms and Armor, *purify food and drink*, *neutralize poison*; **Cost** 9,675 gp

Dagger of the Winter Wonderland

Aura faint conjuration; **CL** 7th; **Price** 11,342 gp; **Weight** 1 lbs.
This strange poniard resembles a carrot perpetually glazed in frost. It functions as a *+1 dagger* but allows the bearer to cast *dimension door* once per day provided they are standing on a patch of snow and reappear on a patch of snow within 360 ft. In addition, the bearer receives a +2-enhancement bonus to all saving throws made against any cold effects or damage.
Feats Craft Magic Arms and Armor, *dimension door*, *endure elements*; **Cost** 5,322 gp

ADVENTURES
WORTH
WINNING